Dalmatian
in a DIGGER

by
Rebecca Elliott

Curious Fox
a capstone company-publishers for children

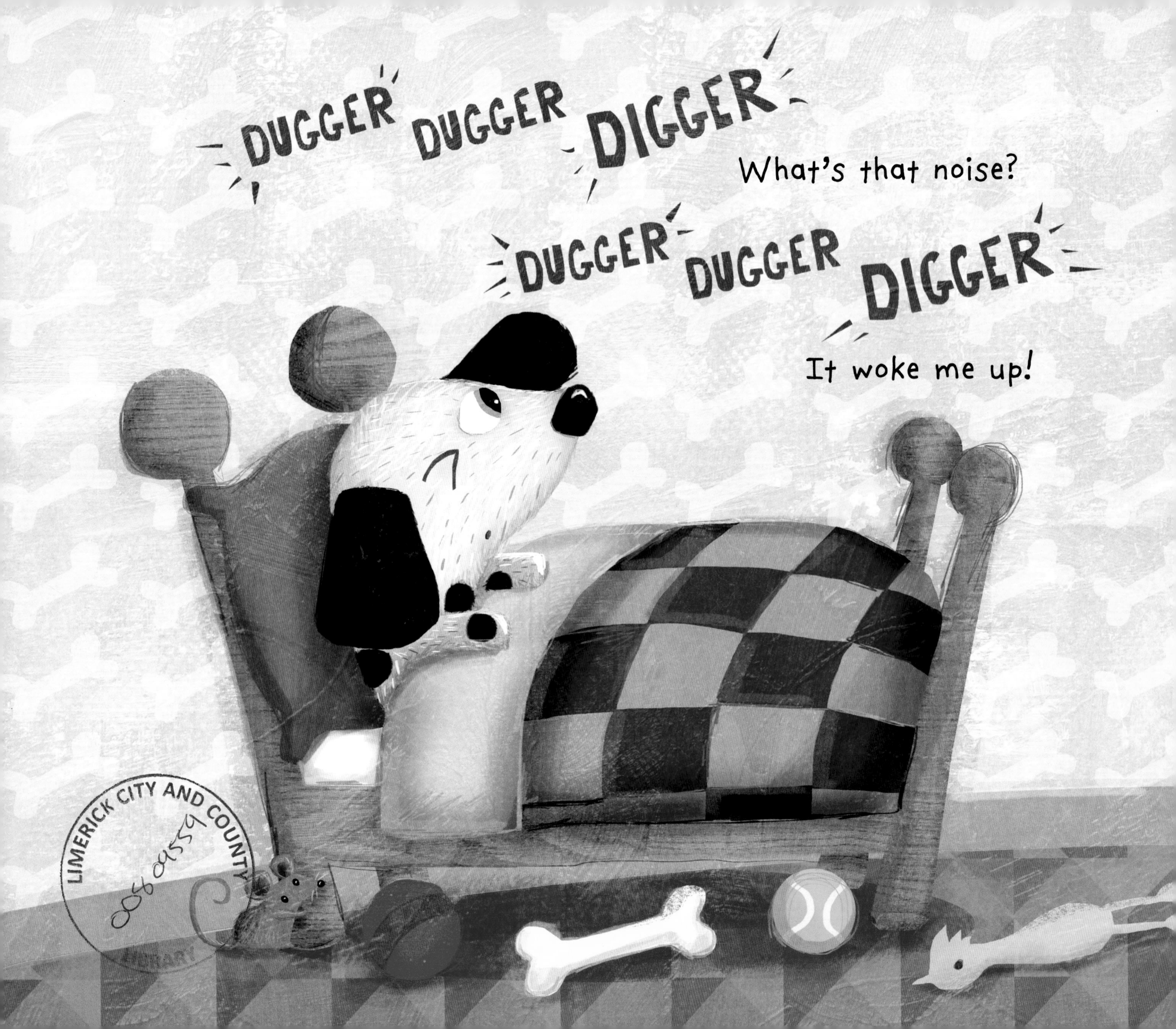

What's that noise?

It woke me up!

He's scooping up dirt.

He's dumping it over there.

BRMMM BRMMM WHEEE

What's THAT noise?

BRMMM BRMMM WHEEE

It really made me jump!

BRMMM BRMMM WHEEE

Oh my! It's a . . .

Camel in a **CRANE!**

BRMMM BRMMM WHEEE

She's picking up the logs.
Then lifting them up high.

BRMMM BRMMM WHEEE

DUMP~SPLAT~CRASH

What's THAT noise?

DUMP~SPLAT~CRASH

It sounds really messy!

DUMP~SPLAT~CRASH

Oh my! It's a . . .

Duck
in a
DUMP
TRUCK!

TUG TUG BEEP

Now what's THAT noise?

TUG TUG BEEP

It sounds really BIG!

TUG TUG BEEP

Oh my! It's a . . .

Bear
in a
BULLDOZER!

He's pushing all the rocks.

TUG TUG BEEP

He's making a huge pile.

TUG TUG BEEP

For Tom and Oli. May you never be too old for dogs and diggers. — R.E.

Published by Curious Fox, an imprint of Capstone Global Library Limited
264 Banbury Road, Oxford, OX2 7DY – Registered company number: 6695582
www.curious-fox.com

Illustrations by Rebecca Elliott

ISBN 978 1 78202 596 2

20 19 18 17 16
10 9 8 7 6 5 4 3 2 1

A CIP catalogue for this book is available from the British Library.

Designer: Lori Bye

Printed and bound in China.